For Daniel

Text copyright © 2004 Fernleigh Books
Illustration copyright © 2004 Piers Harper
All rights reserved. Published by Scholastic Inc.
SCHOLASTIC, CARTWHEEL BOOKS, and associated logos
are trademarks and/or registered trademarks of Scholastic Inc.

ISBN 0-439-57825-6

10 9 8 7 6 5 4 3 2 1   03 04 05 06 07

Printed in China
First printing, 2004

FLUFFY BUNNY

Illustrated by Piers Harper

SCHOLASTIC INC.

Toronto London Auckland Sydney Mexico City New Delhi Hong Kong Buenos Aires

Fluffy Bunny was the very littlest rabbit in his family. And being the very littlest in a very big family wasn't always such fun.

Fluffy Bunny liked to hop and bounce, but his bigger brothers and sisters didn't always let him join in their games. He liked to cuddle up with his mommy and daddy, but they were often too busy.

Sometimes Fluffy Bunny thought no one even remembered he was there.

So, one day, when no one was paying him any mind, he decided to go and find a new family – a family that *always* had time to play with him. Off he hopped, leaving his mommy, his daddy and all his brothers and sisters behind.

Fluffy Bunny hopped and hopped until he heard rustling and scampering noises. He peeped through the golden corn, and there was a family of field mice.

"We're just going home for dinner," they squeaked.
"Come and join us!"
"Maybe this family will look after me," thought
Fluffy Bunny, and he happily skipped away with them.

When they arrived, Mommy Mouse laid out
a meal of nuts and berries for everyone to share.
"Help yourself, Fluffy Bunny," she said.
Fluffy Bunny turned pink to the tips of his ears.

"I'm sorry," he said, "but rabbits can't eat nuts and berries." He remembered how his mommy always fetched him the sweetest grasses and dandelions to eat. "You've been very kind, but I don't think I belong in your family." And he hopped away towards the river.

When he reached the riverbank, he saw
a family of otters rolling and playing together.
Two cubs swam up to him.

"We're playing chase," they called. "Come and
join us!"

"Maybe this family will look after me,"
thought Fluffy Bunny.

But Fluffy Bunny didn't like the otters' splishy splashy river games. He didn't even like getting his feet wet! He remembered the fun he used to have playing hide-and-seek with his brothers and sisters. "I don't think I belong in this family, either," he thought. So he said goodbye and hopped away towards the forest.

Soon he heard a tap, tap, tap in the trees and, looking up, he saw a family of woodpeckers. Two chicks flew down to him.

"We're helping our daddy," they said. "Come and join us!"

"Maybe this family will look after me," thought Fluffy Bunny.

Fluffy Bunny couldn't join in, but seeing the woodpeckers and their daddy reminded him of his own family. He sometimes used to help his daddy to dig in the burrow. He loved doing that!

"It was nice to meet you," he said to the woodpeckers, after a while. "But I don't think I belong in your family." And he hopped away again.

Fluffy Bunny was beginning to think he'd never find a new family when he met some ponies trotting along in the sunshine. He ran to catch up.

"Hello, Fluffy Bunny," the ponies said. "Why don't you run along with us for a while? It's a beautiful sunny day!"

"What fun!" said Fluffy Bunny, and they set off, with the wind rushing through their fur.

But the ponies were much faster than he was, and soon Fluffy Bunny felt tired. He needed to rest.

"Please can we stop?" he called out. But the ponies were so far ahead they couldn't hear him and, in a moment, they were gone.

Poor Fluffy Bunny was left all alone. His ears drooped. None of the families he'd met had been right for him. And the more he thought about his own rabbit family, the more he realized that he missed them.

Then suddenly, Fluffy Bunny saw a group of rabbits hopping over the hill towards him. It was his mommy, his daddy, and all his brothers and sisters!

At last, Fluffy Bunny was safely back home.
"We were so worried about you!" his mommy
said. "Please don't ever go off again."
"I won't," said Fluffy Bunny, sleepily.
"This is where I belong, isn't it?"
"Yes, Fluffy Bunny, it is," said his mommy.
"And we all love you very much."
"I love you, too," said Fluffy Bunny,
and he smiled and closed his eyes.